This Little Tiger book belongs to:
PRESS THE PAGE
HEAR THE NOISE!

LITTLE TIGER PRESS
An imprint of Magi Publications
1 The Coda Centre, 189 Munster Road, London SW6 6AW
www.littletigerpress.com
Produced by Roar Publishing Limited
First published in Great Britain 2012
This edition published 2012

A CIP catalogue record for this book is
available from the British Library

ISBN 978-1-84895-324-6
LTP/1800/0293/0212
Printed in China
2 4 6 8 10 9 7 5 3 1

Little Fin
The Singing Fish

Daren King
with Rebecca Whowell

Gill Guile

LITTLE TIGER PRESS
London

One stormy day, four musical instruments slid off the deck of a ship and tumbled through the water with a . . .

plinketty

plinketty

plonk.

When Little Fin saw the instruments, she wiggled her fins with glee.

“At last I can play in a band!” she cheered, and she swam off to tell her deep-sea friends.

"Come and see! Come and see!" Little Fin called. "Some instruments have fallen from the sky! And I get first pick!"

Off she raced again, her friends chasing behind her.

First Little Fin
tried the drums.

But she could only
hold one drumstick.
"Drums aren't right
for me," she said.

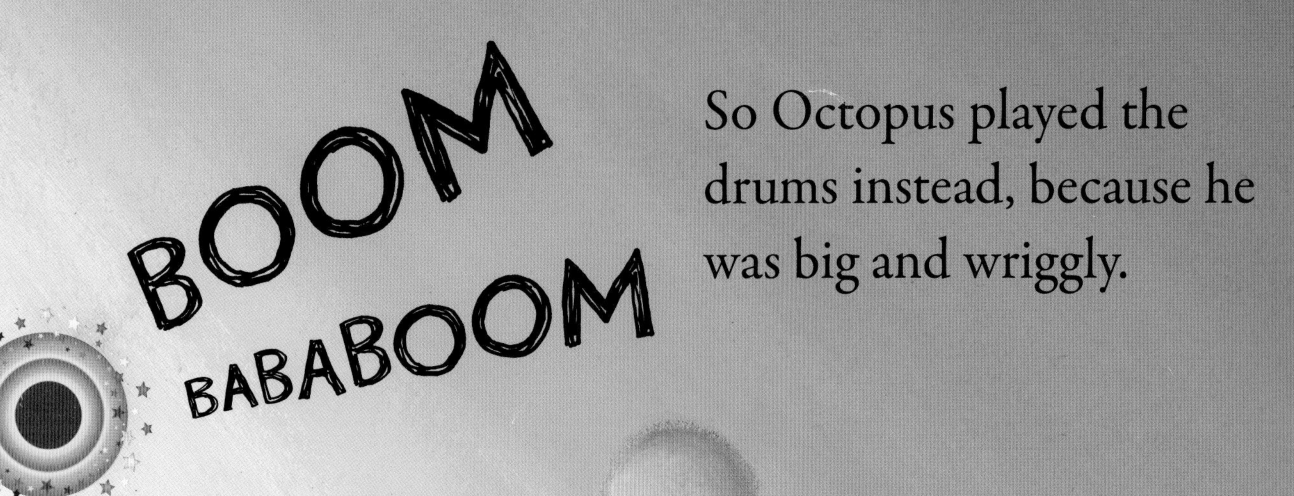
BOOM
BABABOOM

So Octopus played the drums instead, because he was big and wriggly.

So Seahorse played the saxophone because she was a similar shape.

Next Little Fin tried the saxophone. But she didn't have enough puff.

"I'm better at blowing bubbles," she said quietly.

Toodle
oodle
toot

Little Fin tried the piano.
But she was too light to
press the keys.

"This piano is too big!"
she said, a little crossly.

So Starfish went crazy
on the keyboard because he
was tinkly and tumbly.

Tinkle tinkle tinkle

When Little Fin tried the triangle, Whale swished her away with his tail.

"I'm just the right size for this," Whale boomed.

Ting ting ting-a-ling

Little Fin turned a deeper shade of orange. "This is my band," she said, "and there are no instruments left for me!"

But the others were too busy bashing and blowing and plonking and dinging to hear.

Tinkle tinkle

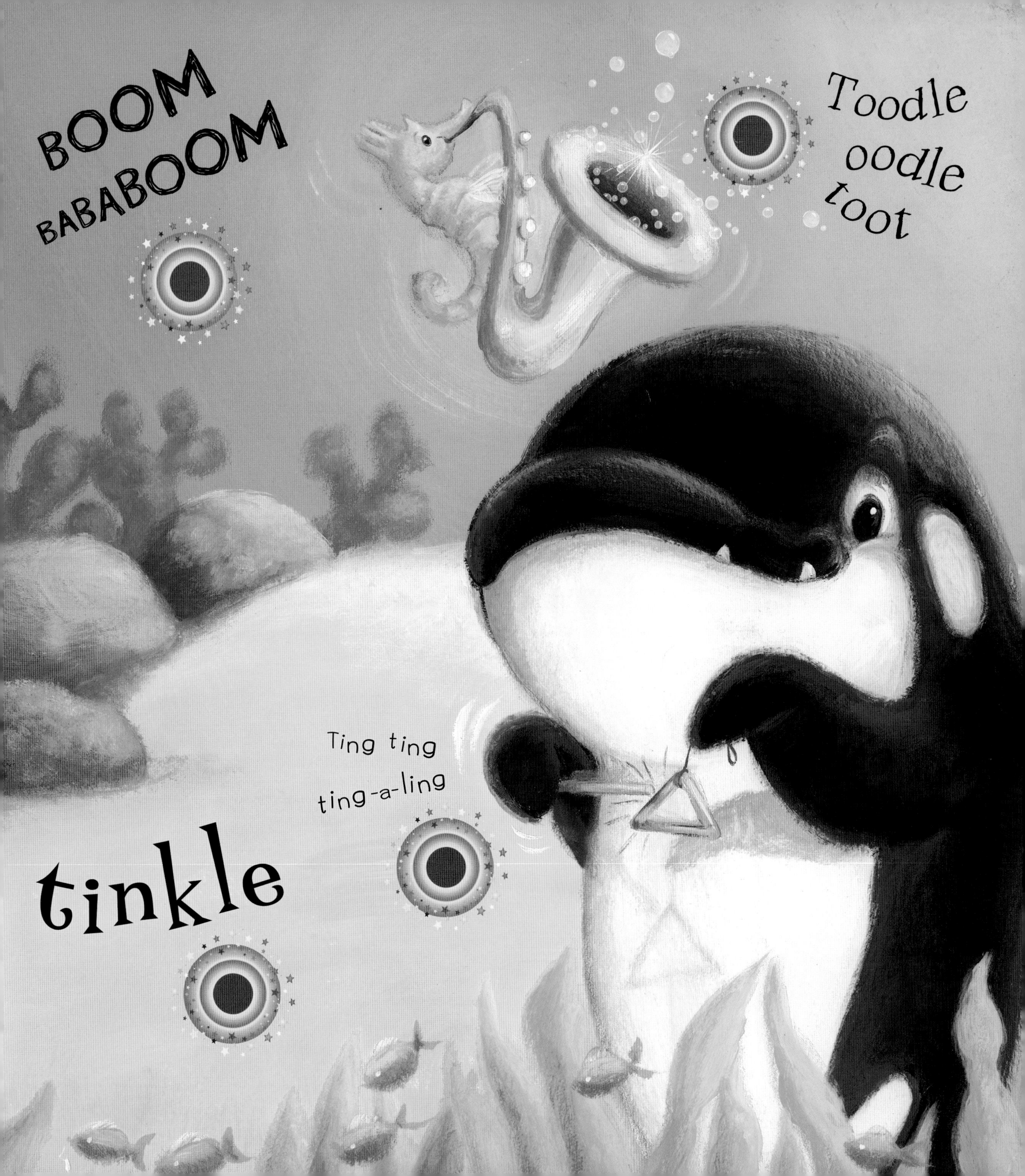
BOOM
BABABOOM
Toodle
oodle
toot
Ting ting
ting-a-ling
tinkle

“I am one of the underwater
unwanted,” said Little Fin.
But nobody heard.

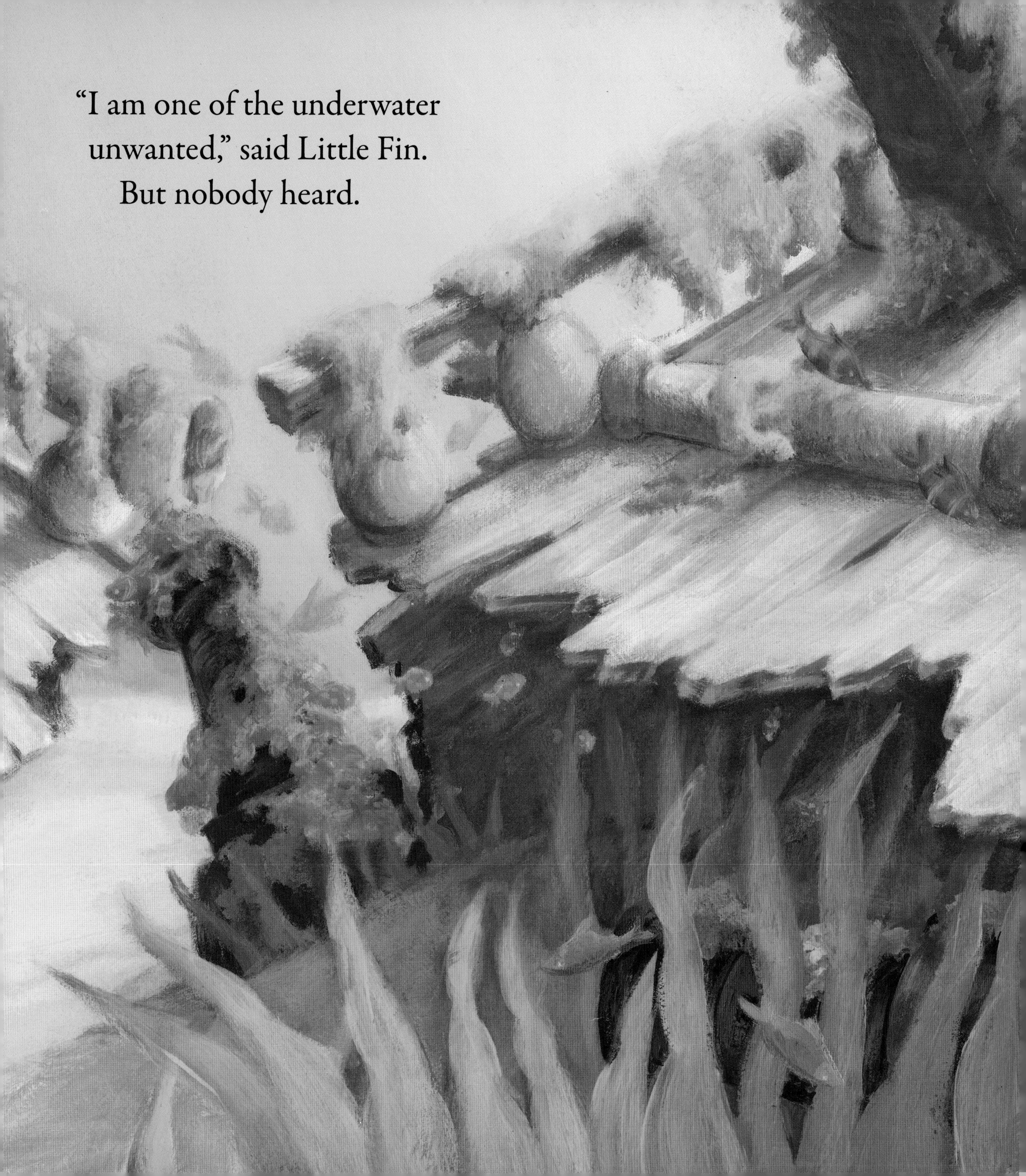

Aah aah aaah

The other animals were still playing away, when Starfish saw some bubbles.

The friends followed the trail until they found Little Fin singing sadly among the reeds.

aaaah aaaaaah!

"We're so sorry for leaving you out," said Seahorse. "You have such a beautiful voice. You should sing in the band!"

"But I wanted to play an instrument," Little Fin said.

"Your voice is the best instrument there is," said Octopus with a smile.

That night, the friends put on a *huge* concert. And the biggest star of the show was Little Fin and her amazing singing!

Toodle
Tinkle
Ting
BOOM
Aaah!

YOU CAN'T MISS THESE VERY NOISY PICTURE BOOKS!

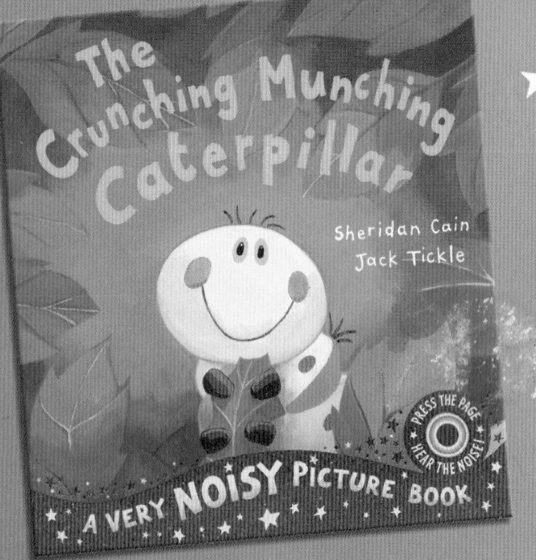
The Crunching Munching Caterpillar
Sheridan Cain
Jack Tickle
PRESS THE PAGE HEAR THE NOISE!
A VERY NOISY PICTURE BOOK

The Noisy Noisy Farm
PRESS THE PAGE HEAR THE NOISE!
A VERY NOISY PICTURE BOOK

WHAT'S THAT NOISE, LITTLE MOUSE?
Stephanie Stansbie
Polona Lovsin
PRESS THE PAGE HEAR THE NOISE!
A VERY NOISY PICTURE BOOK

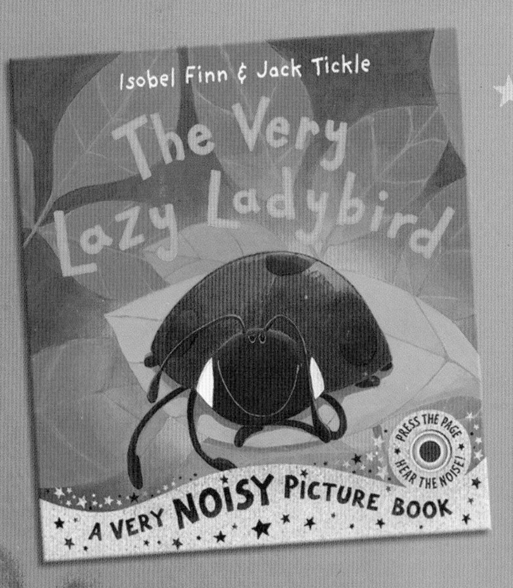
Isobel Finn & Jack Tickle
The Very Lazy Ladybird
PRESS THE PAGE HEAR THE NOISE!
A VERY NOISY PICTURE BOOK

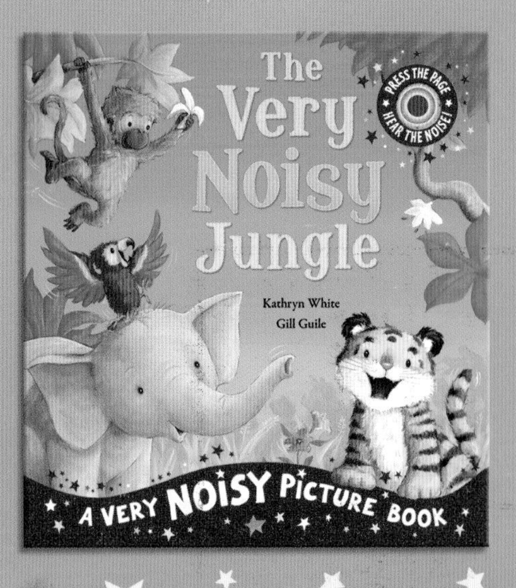
The Very Noisy Jungle
Kathryn White
Gill Guile
PRESS THE PAGE HEAR THE NOISE!
A VERY NOISY PICTURE BOOK

For information regarding any of the above
titles or for our catalogue, please contact us:
Little Tiger Press, 1 The Coda Centre,
189 Munster Road, London SW6 6AW
E-mail: info@littletiger.co.uk • www.littletigerpress.com
Tel: 020 7385 6333 • Fax: 020 7385 7333